Rhymes to Read

The Queen's Day Off

by Sheila May Bird

KN
5/12

Illustrated by Rupert Van Wyk

W

About this book

Rhymes to Read are designed for children who are ready to start reading alone. They can also be used by an adult to share with a child.

The books provide excellent support for developing phonological awareness, helping the child to recognise sounds and sound-symbol relationships. The poems are perfect to read aloud and the strong rhythms, rhymes and repetition will help build confidence and encourage reading and rereading for pleasure.

Reading tips for adults sharing the book with a child:
1. Make reading fun! Choose a time to read when you and the child are relaxed and have time to share the story.
2. Talk about the story before you start reading. Look at the cover and the blurb. What might the story be about? Why might the child like it?
3. Encourage the child to retell the story, using the pictures and rhymes to help. The puzzles at the back of the book provide a good starting point.
4. Give praise! Remember that small mistakes need not always be corrected.
5. For an extra activity you could ask the child to make up some alternative rhymes for the story or their own brand new rhyme!

The Queen looked in her diary.

There was nothing
at all to do.

"I'll take the day off,"
she said.
"So can all of you."

The Queen threw off
her crown, her jewels
and royal frock.

She put on her jeans,
T-shirt, jumper
and socks.

Then she slid down the
banister on to the floor.

It was so much fun that
she did it twice more!

She went to the park
and cycled a bit,

looking for somewhere
comfy to sit.

She had an ice-cream and
a nice sticky bun,

a lolly, some popcorn,

and said, "This is such fun!"

She slid on a slide and
swung on a swing,

then threaded some
daisies into a ring.

She waved to new friends
and as it got dark,

she danced on her tiptoes
all through the park.

Next morning, the Queen said, "I did have such fun."

Then she put on her crown – there was work to be done!

Puzzle 1

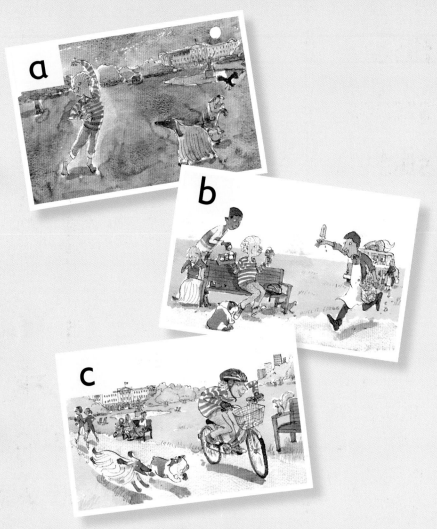

Put the pictures in the correct order and retell the story.

Puzzle 2

floor

stairs

slid

more

fun

work

done

crown

Find the rhyming words above.

Turn over for answers!

Answers

Puzzle 1

The correct order is: c, b, a.

Puzzle 2

The rhyming words are:

a. floor, more

b. done, fun

First published in 2011 by
Franklin Watts
338 Euston Road
London
NW1 3BH

Franklin Watts Australia
Level 17/207 Kent Street
Sydney
NSW 2000

Text © Sheila May Bird 2011
Illustration © Rupert Van Wyk 2011

The rights of Sheila May Bird to be
identified as the author and Rupert Van Wyk
as the illustrator of this Work have been
asserted in accordance with the Copyright,
Designs and Patents Act, 1988.

A CIP catalogue record for this book is
available from the British Library.

ISBN 978 1 4451 0293 1 (hbk)
ISBN 978 1 4451 0299 3 (pbk)

Series Editor: Melanie Palmer
Series Advisor: Catherine Glavina
Series Designer: Peter Scoulding

Printed in China

Franklin Watts is a division of Hachette Children's Books,
an Hachette UK company. www.hachette.co.uk